The Ad
the

The Rescue Of The Dweeble Stone

Karen M Hoyle

Clink Street
London | New York

Published by Clink Street Publishing 2015

First edition.

ISBN: PB: 978-1-910782-49-1
EB: 978-1-910782-50-7

enjoy.

1

STORIES OF MAGICAL CREATURES

Austin awoke early and the suns first rays were just dancing through the gap in the curtains in his bedroom. Austin's wife Mary, whom he loved dearly, was already busy in the kitchen of their little cottage and Austin could smell the Hogs Pudding frying on the stove for his breakfast. Austin jumped out of bed and put on his tatty miners clothes and his strong boots and made his way down to the kitchen, tripping over his snoozing dog 'Bert' on the way. Bert didn't move, just raised an eyebrow and settled back to sleep.

As Austin sat down Mary said, "There are stories Austin, across Cornwall stories are being told about 'The Knockers' and of the meddling Pixies who are always up to mischief. I'm telling you there's magical creatures around the mines, you be on your guard."

Austin was not one to spread these stories and personally felt they could not be true as he had never seen a Pixie or a Knocker. He nodded gently with a smile to Mary,

"Mary I will keep my guard don't you worry I am sure all will be well" he said.

Austin tucked into his spicy sausage meat meal. Bert the dog was now loyally beside him hoping for some sausage to fall his way.

Austin knew the stories as well as anyone. That 'Knockers' are grubby trolls that stand about two feet high, they wear old miners boots and tatty waistcoats and live on the items that miners leave behind. It was believed by all miners to be good luck to throw the crusts of their pasties, that they had eaten for lunch, down to the bottom of the mines where the hungry knockers were said to live. The 'Pixies' were very different, small and could fit in a mans hand, always busy, thinking themselves better than anyone, and enjoyed playing pranks on anyone around.

'No', thought Austin there can't be magical creatures, its was all just tittle tattle.

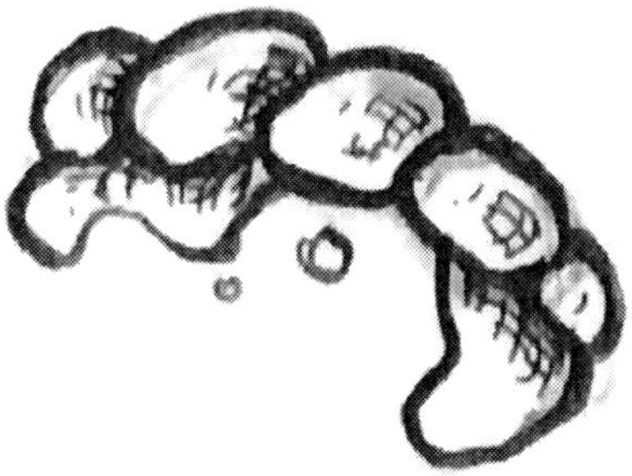

2

THE HIDDEN HAMMER

Breathing in the fresh sea air, Austin walked to work along the clifftop looking out at the St Agnes coast where he would swim every evening on his way home. Swimming was Austin's joy, his time to soak in cool water and he was also the village swimming champion. He worked in a tin mine three hills away but there had been not much tin lately to dig up and the miners were finding it hard to feed their families as they were earning very little money. Austin believed that the stories of magical creatures were a good thing in distracting the people away from a bad situation and could do no real harm. The children would grow up hearing the same stories that he had done when his father first told him of why he should throw his pasty crust away for good luck.

Austin reached the ‘Wheal Coates’ mine entrance. The heavy wooden door was surrounded by purple and yellow glowing heather bushes, Austin smiled and looked forward to seeing their colour on his return to the surface. Austin lit the candle on his helmet, opened the door and began the long walk down into the darkness and whistled his usual tune of ‘Trelawney’ to himself until he reached the rock face where he would work for the day.

Austin dug away at the rock for an hour, and found no tin, just endless black iron rock that had no value or use. Austin kept digging away and his hands began to hurt and his heart sink.

But then, looking closely he could see a golden coloured image start to form in front of him, he dug more and discovered that a golden metal hammer was buried in the rocks. The hammer was beautiful, with a golden head and a oak wood handle with gold and blue coloured stone along its length.

Curious as to how it got there Austin dug it out carefully. He held the hammer up and it glistened in the light of his candle, as it was far better than his own, he started to use it to dig at the rock.

The strangest thing then happened.

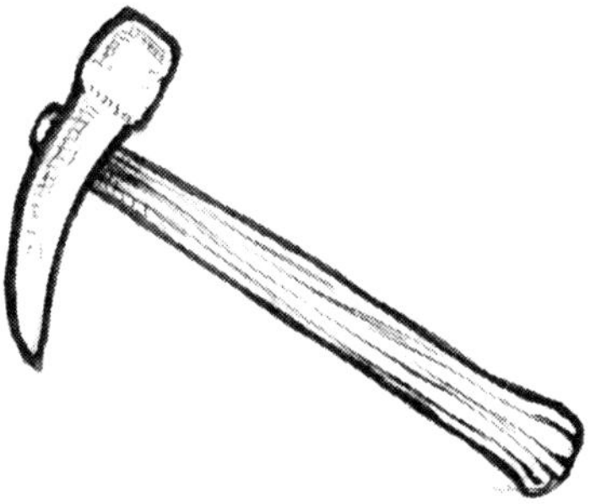

Bang, Bang, Bang… he hit the rock three times with the new hammer and the rock in front of him vanished into thin air.

3

THE KNOCKERS CAVERN

Austin rubbed his eyes twice as he could not believe what he was seeing. He was no longer in his mine tunnel, he was now in a cavern where the walls twinkled with blue stones, some of the stones were as big as his hand and he could see the reflection of his helmet candle in them. He looked to the far side of the cavern and there they were, they did exist, 'Knockers' really were sitting around a table eating the pasty crusts that had been thrown down by the miners.

Austin was suddenly scared. The Knockers turned and looked at Austin and then with big smiles, cheered and all together shouted "Welcome."

Austin felt himself smile and weakly he began to introduce himself.

Karen M Hoyle

"Er…um…hello…I'm Austin…"

To his surprise they waved to him to join them for food. He walked over and sat on a very small stool made from old miner's hats. Half eaten pasties with blackberries and apples at one end and meat and potato at the other lay on the table. As he looked he could clearly see the black miner's finger marks on the pasty crusts. Suddenly one of the knockers spoke to him.

“So when are you going then?”

Shocked that they spoke as humans do, Austin stuttered a reply;

“Going? Going where?”

The Knocker pointed at a hole at the side of the cavern;

“To the Silver Lakes to get The Dweeble?”

Still confused Austin replied; "Who or what is The Dweeble?"

"Blimey!, Dweeble, Dweeble Stone?… no…no wiser?…The Dweeble Stone is the magic stone that you have to rescue…You have to rescue the stone."

The Knocker threw a pasty crust over his shoulder narrowly missing another Knocker who ducked just in time.

"No...I don't rescue stones...I'm just a miner, I just dig things... I'm leaving in a minute...got tin to dig...I do digging" Austin found himself doing digging motions with his hands then decided to bury his hands in his pockets to stop himself feeling so silly.

The Knocker laughed loudly; "Don't think so... and you certainly won't have any tin to dig up..."

Austin turned; "What? Why do you know that?

"Have you not noticed that when you are mining you are not finding any tin to dig up? Well that's because The Dweeble Stone has gone, The Dweeble Stone is magic because it turns rock into Tin."

Getting curious Austin moved towards the Knocker; "And you have lost this stone?"

Backing off, the Knocker cleared his throat before continuing; "Yes and for us The Dweeble Stone also turns rock into these blue stones. You see the shining blue rocks in the walls… we sell these to the Pixies. The Pixies thought it was a funny joke to take The Dweeble Stone and see if they can make their own blue stones so they don't have to buy them from us. The problem is they don't know what to do with The Dweeble Stone to make it work, only a Knocker can cast the right words to make it work. Therefore we win!"

Coming out from behind the pasty table another Knocker shouted out; "How can we be winning when we have lost The Dweeble?, you are such a fool Deffler."

Austin gave a little smile as he agreed with the second Knockers comments, but he was still trying to believe the situation he was now in.

"So, Deffler…You still haven't told me why you need me, why don't you just go to the Silver Lakes and get it yourself?" said Austin.

"Well you see those mushroom hopping Pixies have hidden it in one of the lakes, and we Knockers can't swim, we just sink! We put that hammer in the rock to get a miner here to help us. We know you can swim, we've seen you do it". Deffler looked triumphant.

“I wondered why the hammer was just there…how do you know I can swim?, not all humans can you know!” Austin said raising his voice.

The Knockers all looked shocked and Deffler fell off the rock he was standing on. “What!!!” then it was silent.

Austin shook his head and was first to speak, “As it happens I can swim, but I don’t know about all the rest of this rescue stuff, this is your problem not mine."

"Well if you want no tin to dig up that's fine. Of course that means you'll have no money to live on or food to feed your families." Deffler looked very sure of himself.

Austin imagined his lovely wife back at their cottage an the people of the village who were struggling to survive. He turned to Deffler; "Ok I'll do it, but you promise to make sure that there will be plenty of tin to keep me and the other miners in a good life afterwards."

Excited, Deffler rose back to his full

height of two feet and one inch; "We can give you more than that, we can produce blue stones for you as well, you miners don't have any blue stones do you?…think how rich you can be with blue stone and the tin."

Austin leaned forward and grabbed Deffler by the collar of his shabby waistcoat and lifted him slightly off the ground "Not bothered about being rich, just need enough to keep everyone happy, which we were before you Knockers lost The Dweeble Stone in the first place!!… it is because of you that we have no money, so I'd say it's the least you can do for my help!"

"Yes of course…we are sorry" said Deffler as his legs searched desperately for the ground.

Two hours had passed and Deffler was trying for the fifth time to put a back pack over his small shoulders without falling over. The Knockers had filled the back pack with two hammers, ten large crusts of pasty and a large bottle of water. This was all for the journey to the Silver Lakes, and made Austin wonder just how far they were going. There was a loud thud as the rucksack once again hit the floor.

"Oh for the love of Thunder!, give it to me" said Austin. He picked up the rucksack and neatly slipped it over one shoulder. "Just how far are we going?"

4

THE JOURNEY BEGINS

"Only a couple of hours" said Deffler.

"Then why enough food for a week?" quizzed Austin.

"Oh its not for us, ha, no no, well maybe one little crust...but no no... its for Maggie!" laughed Deffler.

"Who's Maggie?" asked Austin.

“Maggie is the mad old pixie who will get us to the Silver Lakes. She runs a rather interesting Pixie Bed and Breakfast. She had a falling out with the Pixies a while back and now lives on her own on the edge of the lakes. We send her the odd scraps of crusts we don’t need, she can have a nasty temper some times, poor Denzel over there got his ears turned into fish for three days, didn’t half smell I can tell you!” said Deffler pointing and holding his nose.

"But will she help us?" said Austin.

"Yes, this gives her a chance to get back at the pixies…" Deffler finished doing up his waistcoat and picked up a candle. He waved his arm in the direction of a hole in the wall of the cavern and Austin followed as they entered into the darkness.

5

MEETING MAGGIE

After a long time in the dark, Austin and Deffler walked out onto a meadow of the greenest grass Austin had ever seen. The sun was bright and the flowers seemed to be humming happy tunes to themselves. Ahead was a wooden shack that was only about as high as Deffler, and a grand looking pixie with grey hair under a golden head band was sitting on a mushroom looking annoyed. As they walked closer she shouted out;

“Well it took you long enough Deffler!, The Pixies have been celebrating for weeks now. Taking your Dweeble Stone is the biggest thing they have done in years.”

“We had to get the right help Maggie, we needed someone to swim, and here he is. Maggie this is Austin, Austin this is…"

"Maggie Farrenworth Fopp" said Maggie holding out a tiny hand, owner of the finest Pixie Bed and Breakfast in these lands. Right now that is out of the way, can we get going Deffler?"

Austin removed his hand swiftly from Maggie's and tried to ignore her rudeness.

"Yes I would like nothing more Maggie, I'll leave these here for you" Deffler put the contents of the rucksack of crusts and water into the wooden shack and rejoined Maggie and Austin. "Off we go then."

Deffler then muttered "ungrateful old so and so" under his breathe.

Maggie flicked her wrist at Deffler, "I heard that!" suddenly Deffler's fingers had turned into worms and he couldn't stop them wriggling.

"Hey stop it! I need those to climb the ladder!" screamed Deffler, Maggie huffed and put Defflers fingers back to normal.

Soon they were all at the bottom of a silver ladder that led up to a cave. Maggie went first followed by Austin and Deffler and the three of them stood facing a silvery wall of rock. Deffler took out the two hammers he still had in the rucksack and gave one to Austin.

“Three times remember” said Deffler. Bang, Bang, Bang. Austin and Deffler hit the wall of silver with their hammers and as before Austin found himself not where he started. He was now in a meadow of grass, except the grass was silver in colour and the most beautiful blue lake Austin had ever seen stretched out before him.

6
THE LAKES

"Wow" said Austin.

"Wow in deed" said Deffler "We haven't seen one pesky pixie yet!"

"They'll be around" said Maggie "They'll be guarding The Dweeble Stone, don't you worry."

“Where is the Silver Lake?” asked Austin.

“The Silver Lake is inside that Blue Lake” said Maggie pointing.

Austin found himself saying “What?” for the hundredth time that day.

“Once you go below the water’s surface you will see it. You will need to swim down to it. Careful though the current in the silver lake is strong and will pull you all over. The Dweeble Stone is at the bottom in a box". Maggie turned and was gone, back through the wall they had just come through, leaving Austin with his mouth still open and Deffler sitting on the silver grass scratching his head.

"Is she always like that?" said Austin

"Yes, never one to hang around is Maggie!. Tricky this is now, very tricky…" Deffler looked like he was thinking hard.

"So…should I just jump in then?." said Austin.

"Think so." said Deffler.

Austin stood at the edge of the water and just as he was about to jump in three Pixies appeared in front of him.

"Ha!! got you!…who are you?" said a pink Pixie.

"Um…no-one…just popped by for a swim" said Austin trying to smile…

"You can't just have popped by for a swim here…its secret!, no-one knows this place except us" said a blue pixie.

"Well its not so secret is it? said Austin " Because here I am."

The pixies looked at each other confused.

Suddenly Deffler sneezed from behind the rock he was hiding behind.

"Knew it!! Knew it!!! Knocker, Knocker!!!" shouted the three pixies all together.

Austin grabbed his mining helmet that was on the floor next to him and put it over the three pixies trapping them inside it; he banged it into the ground with his boot and looked back at Deffler.

"We'd better hurry others may have heard that." said Austin.

"Yes, quick then quick!!" said Deffler. The pixie's yells could quietly be heard under the helmet.

Austin threw himself forwards into the water in more of a jump than a dive. He found it easy to fall through the water and quickly he could see the Silver Lake below him. He kicked hard in the warm water but as he reached the Silver Lake he suddenly felt very cold, and his lungs hurt as he swam harder in the Silver Lakes' current.

After what seemed like a very long time and just as he was getting dizzy he saw a small box on the floor of the lake. He reached forward with all his strength and picked up the box, it ripped from his reach in the current and Austin had to swing his arms to catch again. He had no breathe left to check if the stone was actually in the box, he kicked hard for the surface. With a splash his head re-appeared above the water, Deffler was on the shore waving at him madly. Clearing the water from his eyes he swam to towards where Deffler was standing.

As he pulled himself out of the water he could hear a breeze, then looking up he realised that it was not the wind, but a thousand pixie voices chattering around him. He tightened his grip on the box, Deffler ran up to him.

"Easy now, easy….keep smiling." Deffler nodded to the pixie crowd in front of him.

"So you have the stone do you?" said a senior looking Pixie.

"What?" said Austin trying to look innocent.

"We saw you swim down, we see the box in your hand" said the Pixie

Austin put the box into his pocket, "Yes! I saw the old thing when I was swimming, I just thought the box would be handy to put my dominoes in, I like my dominoes I do."

Deffler thought it best to stay quiet.

"Likely story", said the Pixie "Show us the box."

Austin pulled the box from his pocket "Yes here it is, nice little thing."

"Open it and we shall see what you were really after" pushed the now grumpy pixie

Deffler tried to stop him, but Austin opened the box and showed it to all the pixies staring at him.

The pixies gasped and shook their heads.

Deffler looked at the box and it was

empty, he covered his eyes, they had failed, there was no Dweeble Stone and they been caught by the pixies, it couldn't be worse.

"So can we go then?" asked Austin "That's if you don't mind me having the box?, finders keepers and all that."

"I suppose we have no reason to doubt you. Go then." The Pixie pointed to five of the larger looking pixies to form a guard around the blue lake. Austin and Deffler walked back to the rocks where they had appeared from when they arrived.

"Bye then, nice to meet you" Austin shouted back to the pixies as he picked up his hammer.

Bang, Bang, Bang… The silver rocks disappeared and they were both transported back to outside Maggies wooden shack.

7

RETURNING TO THE CAVERN

Deffler slumped on the grass, his head in his hands.

"What's up with you?" said Austin " The Pixies let us go."

"Yes, but we don't have the stone, the Dweeble Stone… we've blown it, blown it!, no more Tin for you either!"

Austin smiled and reached into his pocket, he opened his hand and showed Deffler a glowing blue and gold rock.

"Do you mean this stone?"

"That's it, that's it!! The Dweeble... How...?" screamed Deffler

"I put it into my pocket as I took the box out, I knew we would be okay"

Deffler threw his arms around Austin's neck and gave him a big sloppy kiss on the cheek.

“Hey!, …get off!!” said Austin, Deffler started dancing around on the grass.

After eating a feast of pasty crusts covered in sugary syrup and cream, Austin waved goodbye to the Knockers in their cavern. The twinkling blue stones in the walls seemed to glow brighter, The Dweeble Stone had been returned to its rightful place in a small hole in the rock at the top of the cavern.

Austin hit the cavern wall three times with the hammer.

Bang, Bang, Bang…He was back in his mining tunnel, he smiled to himself and thought:

"Just wait until I tell Mary, she was right all along."

Austin could hear shouts and cheers further up the tunnel and the mine bell was ringing loudly. As he walked further he could see men hugging each other and dancing in the tunnels.

Austin climbed back up the mine tunnel and into daylight, he tucked his new hammer safely in his belt so not to lose it. All around him miners and their wives were celebrating and holding lumps of orange coloured Tin rock. The Tin was back, the villagers would feed their families and have money again. The Dweeble Stone was truly magical.

The walk home was a happy one, and he felt he had done enough swimming for one day as he looked out to sea. As he reached the front door of his house, there on the doorstep was a bag of pasty crusts and a wonderful stool made of old miners helmets with a note that read in untidy writing;

"Thank you, from Deffler and your new friends."

The end (for now)

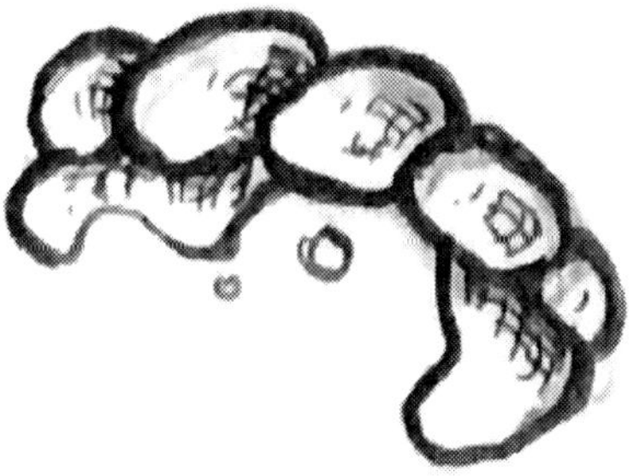

More adventures for Austin are yet to come…

To sign up for the next books

in the series visit

www.theadventuresofaustin.com

About the Author: Born in Newquay Cornwall, Karen M Hoyle has written since the age of 11 when her first poem was published. Having also developed television scripts and having a career in Marketing and Public Relations, Karen made sure writing was always at the centre of her life. 'The Rescue of The Dweeble Stone' was first drafted in 2004 and was put to one side for editing, finally eleven years later in 2015 the book has been brought back to life and Austin's Adventures are about to begin and relight the imagination of both author and reader. This is the first book of a five part series exploring and opening up Cornwall's magical backdrop to children and adults alike.

Lightning Source UK Ltd.
Milton Keynes UK
UKOW02f1552230915

259122UK00002B/22/P

9 781910 782491